WE'VE GOT TALENT

HANNAH WHITTY

PAULA BOWLES

SIMON & SCHUSTER

London   New York   Sydney   Toronto   New Delhi

It was Olivia's most favourite time of year –
it was time for the school play.
"Calm down!" laughed Mummy.

"But I can't calm down!" Olivia cried. "I'm too excited!
This year the play is about a princess **and** a knight!"
And she hopped off to prepare for the big audition.

At Sam's house there was also a lot of excitement –
he had never been in a play before.
"Dad, Dad!" Sam cried. "This year the school
play is about a knight, a princess **and** a dragon!
I'm going to audition!"

And with that, he hurried upstairs to practise.

Sam practised as
hard as he could.

He practised in
front of the mirror.

He practised in the bath.

He even practised in Mr Pythagoras's maths class!

Over at Olivia's house there was a lot of noise . . .

"What's all that hullabaloo?!" asked Mummy,
poking her head around the door.
"I'm practising my stage voice!" announced Olivia.

Finally, the big day arrived – it was audition day.
Sam was a bit nervous but his dance moves were spectacular!

Olivia wasn't nervous at all
and said all her lines perfectly.

"Well done, everyone!" said Miss Binks.
"The parts will be announced tomorrow."

That night, Sam and Olivia lay wide awake.
I hope I get the part I want, thought Sam.

DANCING STARS

Olivia was practising her very best delighted face. I need to be prepared for when I get the part I want, she thought.

STAR TODAY

The next morning the parts were put up on a big list in the school assembly hall.

AFTER SCHOOL CLUBS

Mon: Art Club

Tues: Science Club

Weds: Sports Club

Thurs: Games Club

Fri: Book Club

Big City Primary School presents...

The Princess, The Knight, and the Dragon

Friday 2 p.m.

School Hall

CAST LIST

Brave Sir Knight ....Sam

Dancing Princess ....Olivia

Dragon .... Toby

Queen .... Rose

King .... Leo

Townsfolk .... Marc, Viki, Jennifer, Jason, Ruth, Laura, Michael, Angela

Sheep .... Beth, Chloe, Mark, Katie, Jacob, Milo

Lunch Menu

Fish and Chips
Macaroni Cheese
Rice Pudding
Fruit Salad

SUPERKITTY SCHOOL VISIT

MONDAY 10 a.m.

"**Oh?**" said Sam, sadly.
"But I REALLY wanted to be the princess."

"**Oh?**" said Olivia, crossly.
"I'm SUPPOSED to be
the knight!"

In rehearsals, Sam put on the knight's costume
and tried out some of his best dance moves.
But it was no use.

The costume was too heavy and the sword
got in the way. It just didn't feel right.

When Olivia stared at the script she was horrified.
The princess had no lines – she just danced!
Olivia tried to talk but . . .

"The pretty princess dances so gracefully,"
said Miss Binks. "She doesn't need to speak!"
Well . . . THAT didn't feel right at all!

Sam watched Olivia as she attempted a twirl and fell over.

"Are you OK?" he asked.

"Yes," said Olivia.
"I just really **don't** like dancing."

Sam couldn't believe it!
"I **love** dancing!"
he cried. "It's the
most magical feeling
in the world!

But my part doesn't
have any dancing, just
lots of words to say.
Speaking in front of all
those people is scary!"

"Sam," said Olivia, smiling suddenly. "I've got an idea!" So together they hatched a plan . . .

After weeks of rehearsals,
the opening night finally came!

The stage was set, the lights ready,
the audience hushed, and then . . .

. . . the curtain lifted.

"This is the story of a very smart and very brave princess!"
announced Olivia, adjusting her crown and her sword.
"And the most talented, and most amazing, dancing knight!"

Sam leapt onto the stage in his sparkling tutu and shiny knight's helmet. He gave the most spectacular twirl and the play began.

The audience gasped as Sam danced beautifully,

and they cheered as Olivia spoke her lines perfectly.

Together, the very smart, very brave princess
and the amazing, dancing knight defeated
the big, bad dragon and saved the day.

"Olivia, you were **brilliant!**" said her mummy after the play, giving her a big hug.

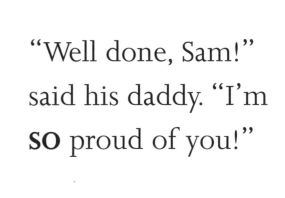

"Well done, Sam!" said his daddy. "I'm **SO** proud of you!"

Just then, Miss Binks thundered over.
"Uh-oh," said Sam. "Uh-oh," said Olivia.
They were certainly in trouble now!

"I loved it!" said Miss Binks.

And so did everyone else . . .
HOORAY!